ABDO Publishing Company is the exclusive school and library distributor of Rabbit Ears Books.

Library bound edition 2005.

Library of Congress Cataloging-in-Publication Data

Roberts, Tom, 1944-.
  The three billy goats Gruff / adapted by Tom Roberts ; illustrated by David Jorgensen.
      p. cm.
  "Rabbit Ears books."
  Summary: Three clever billy goats outwit a big, ugly troll that lives under the bridge they must cross on their way up the mountain.
  ISBN 1-59197-754-1
  [1. Fairy tales. 2. Folklore—Norway.] I. Jorgensen, David, ill. II. Asbjørnsen, Peter Christen, 1812-1885. Tre bukkene Bruse. English. III. Title.

PZ8.R524Tf 2004
398.2'09481'04529648—dc22

                                                        2004045389

All Rabbit Ears books are reinforced library binding
and manufactured in the United States of America.

adapted by Tom Roberts

The Three Billy Goats Gruff

illustrated by David Jorgensen

Rabbit Ears Books

Three billy goats, so the story goes, were grazing in a fresh, fragrant field, munching on grass and thinking of finer things.

"Grrrufff," snapped the biggest billy goat, ripping up some turf.

"Grrrufff, grrrufff," chomped the middle billy goat, gnashing some arugula.

"Grrrufff, grrrufff, grrrufff," bleated the youngest billy goat, not to be outdone.

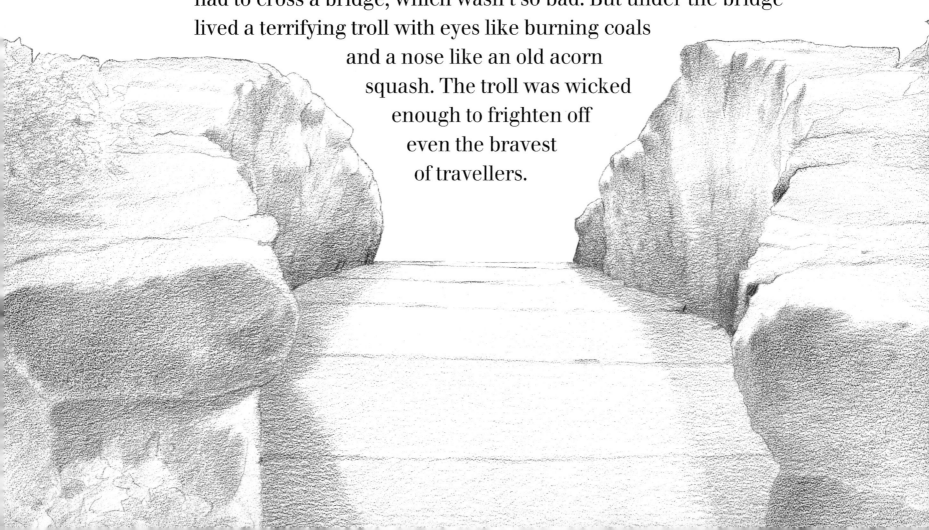

To no one's surprise, the three billy goats called themselves
Gruff. And truth to tell, all three yearned to graze on the greens in
the meadow of clover across the river. But to get over there, they
had to cross a bridge, which wasn't so bad. But under the bridge
lived a terrifying troll with eyes like burning coals
and a nose like an old acorn
squash. The troll was wicked
enough to frighten off
even the bravest
of travellers.

The youngest billy goat Gruff, lulled by the lure of finer fields, stepped onto the bridge. "Clip-clop," went his little hooves. Up sprang the troll.

"Who dares to clip-clop over my bridge?" fumed the troll.

"It's only I, Mr. Troll, the youngest billy goat Gruff, crossing over to finer fields," said the little goat in a tiny voice.

"Billy Goat for breakfast! Billy Goat for lunch! I shall eat you up," slobbered the troll, licking his puffy lips.

"Oh don't bother with me," squealed the youngest billy goat Gruff. "My brother's crossing behind me and he's much more to your liking."

The troll's great nose quivered as he thought. Then his eyes blazed bright as he said, "Go your way then. I shall bide my time."

And the youngest billy goat Gruff clip-clopped across the bridge and into the meadow of clover.

Later on, the middle billy goat Gruff stepped onto the bridge. "Clip-clop", went his medium-sized hooves. Up sprang the troll.

"Who dares to clip-clop over my bridge?" roared the troll.

"It's only me, Mr. Troll, the middle billy goat Gruff, crossing over to greener grass," said the middle goat in a medium sort of voice.

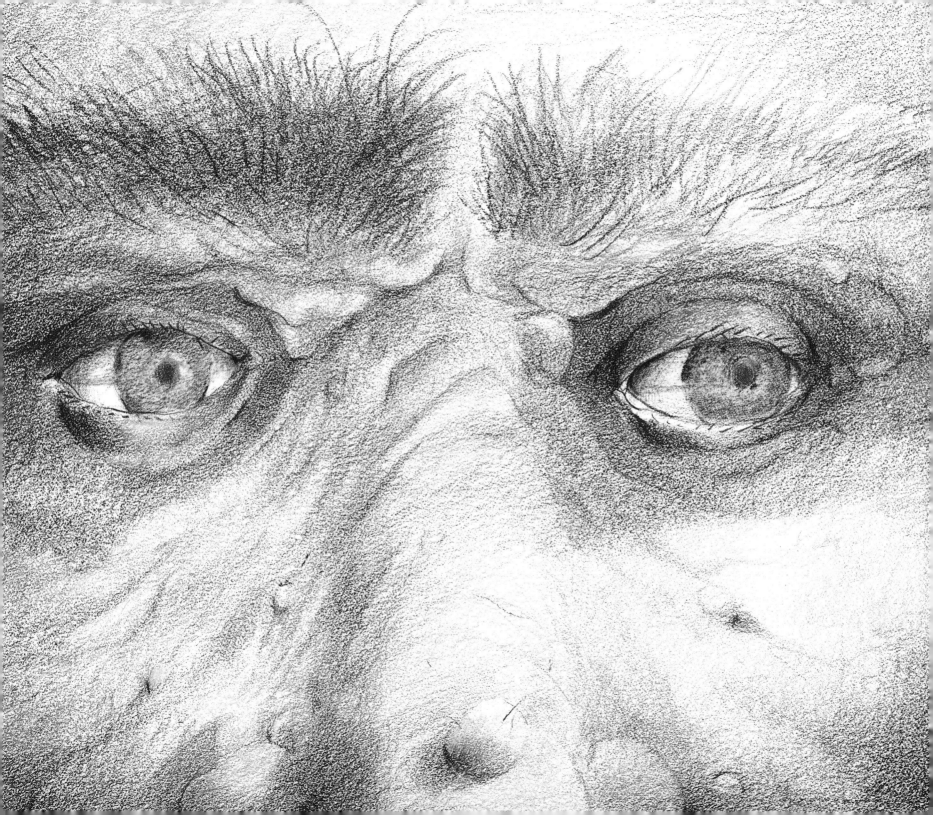

"Billy goat for breakfast! Billy goat for lunch! I shall eat you up," trilled the troll, rubbing his bloated belly.

"Oh please man, leave me alone," said the middle billy goat Gruff. "My brother's crossing behind me. He's much more of a meal for you."

The troll thought again, tapped his nose and hefted his belly. "Go your way then. I shall bide my time."

And the middle billy goat Gruff clip-clopped across the bridge and into the meadow of clover.

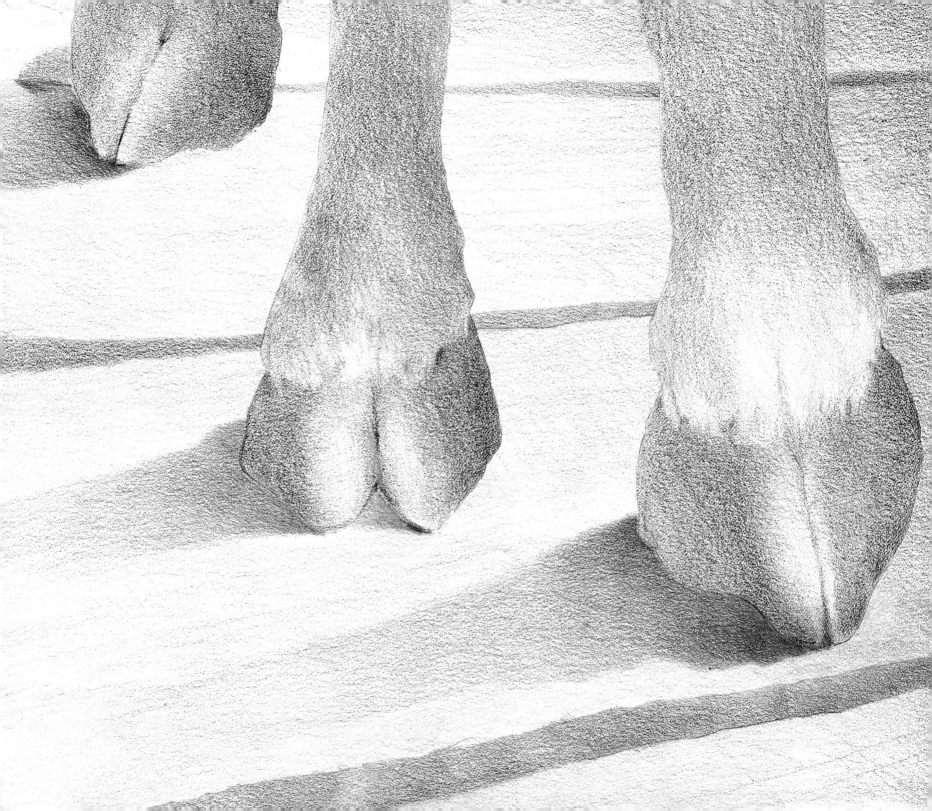

Shortly after that, the biggest billy goat Gruff stepped onto the bridge. "CLIP-CLOP," went his big hooves, and the bridge groaned under his weight.

Up sprang the troll. "Who dares to clip-clop over my bridge?" bellowed the troll.

"It's only I, Mr. Troll, the biggest billy goat Gruff, crossing over to more verdant victuals."

"Billy goat for breakfast! Billy goat for lunch! Billy goat, billy goat, munch munch munch. I shall eat you up."

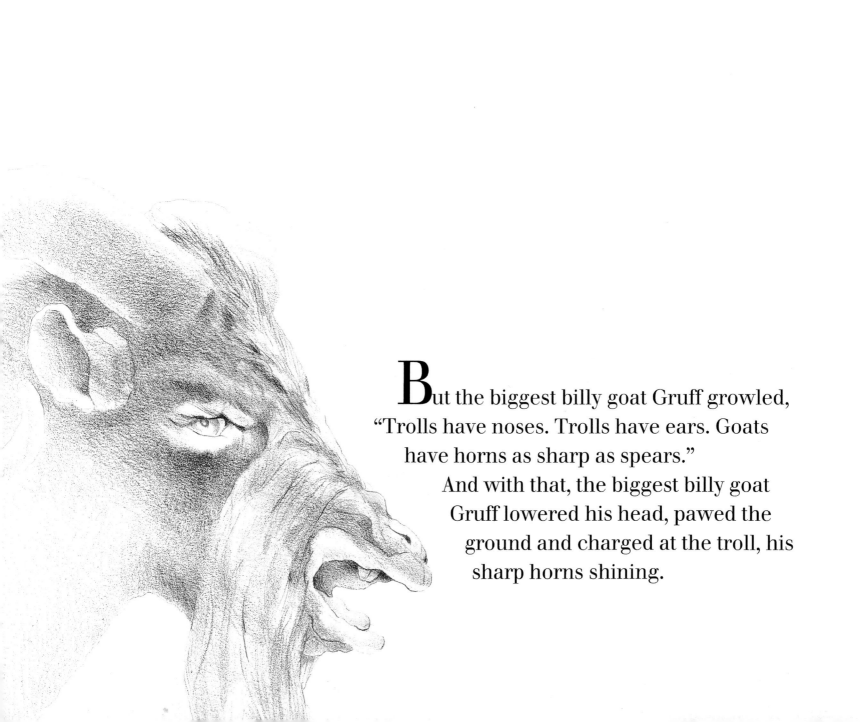

But the biggest billy goat Gruff growled, "Trolls have noses. Trolls have ears. Goats have horns as sharp as spears."

And with that, the biggest billy goat Gruff lowered his head, pawed the ground and charged at the troll, his sharp horns shining.

He butted the troll up, up in the air, over the bridge, and into the river. The troll sank like a stone and was never seen again.

The three billy goats Gruff, so we're told, are still there grazing in both fields now, and growing fatter every day.